Born to Ride

A Story About Bicycle Face

Story by **Larissa Theule**

Pictures by **Kelsey Garrity-Riley**

Abrams Books for Young Readers • New York

For my mom and dad
—L.T.

For Eliza
—K.G.R.

Library of Congress Cataloging-in-Publication Data

Names: Theule, Larissa, author. | Garrity-Riley, Kelsey, illustrator.
Title: Born to Ride / by Larissa Theule; illustrations, Kelsey Garrity-Riley.
Description: New York: Abrams Books for Young Readers, 2019. | Summary: In Rochester, New York, in 1896, Louisa Belinda Bellflower defies convention and ignores her brother's warnings by learning to ride a bicycle. Includes a history of bicycling and its connection to the women's rights movement.
Identifiers: LCCN 2018023154 (print) | LCCN 2018029239 (ebook) | ISBN 978-1-6833-5459-8 (All e-books) | ISBN 978-1-4197-3412-0 (hardcover with jacket : alk. paper)
Subjects: | CYAC: Bicycles and bicycling—Fiction. | Sex role—Fiction. | Brothers and sisters—Fiction. | Family life—New York—Rochester—Fiction. | Rochester (N.Y.)—History—19th century—Fiction.
Classification: LCC PZ7.T3526 (ebook) | LCC PZ7.T3526 Bic 2019 (print) | DDC [E]—dc23

Text copyright © 2019 Larissa Theule
Illustrations copyright © 2019 Kelsey Garrity-Riley
Book design by Pamela Notarantonio

The Susan B. Anthony quote (*opposite*) appeared in the *New York World* on February 2, 1896.
The interview with Susan B. Anthony was conducted by Nellie Bly.

Printed and bound in China
10 9 8 7 6 5 4 3 2 1

Abrams Books for Young Readers are available at special discounts when purchased in quantity for premiums and promotions as well as fundraising or educational use. Special editions can also be created to specification. For details, contact specialsales@abramsbooks.com or the address below.

Abrams® is a registered trademark of Harry N. Abrams, Inc.

ABRAMS The Art of Books
195 Broadway, New York, NY 10007
abramsbooks.com

Let me tell you what I think of bicycling. I think it has done more to emancipate women than anything else in the world. I stand and rejoice every time I see a woman ride by on a wheel.

—SUSAN B. ANTHONY

In Rochester, New York, in the year 1896, girls and women
lived by a long list of things they were told not to do.
They were not to vote, for example; that was against the law.
They were also told not to wear pants or ride a bicycle.

But Louisa Belinda Bellflower had a mind to ride a bicycle no matter what anyone might say.

Her brother, Joe, had been given a brand-new Van Cleve, and riding it looked like a whole lot of fun.

This was Louisa Belinda
Bellflower's everyday outfit.

Not comfortable,
I think you will agree.

This was Joe's
everyday outfit.

Also not comfortable, but at
least one could cartwheel in it.

Louisa Belinda cast aside her skirts
and put on her brother's pants.

"Teach me to ride," she said.

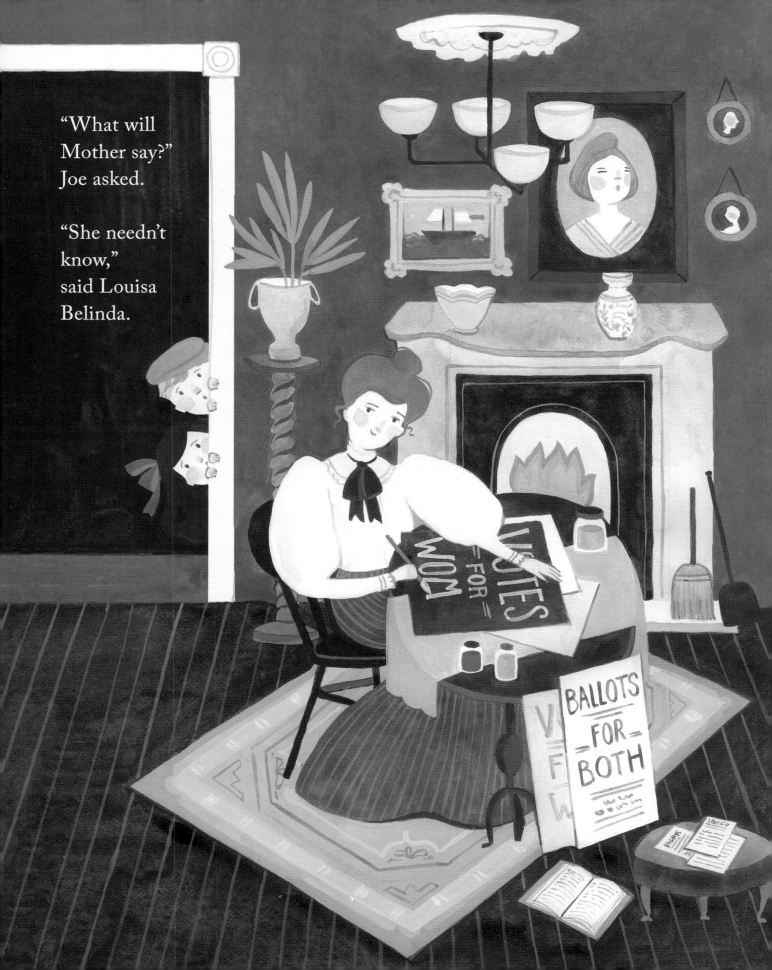

"What will
Mother say?"
Joe asked.

"She needn't
know,"
said Louisa
Belinda.

"But what about—" Joe lowered his voice, "*bicycle face*? It's real, you know, everyone says so, even Dr. Brown."

"He says girls aren't strong enough to balance, that your eyes will bulge, and your jaw will close up from the strain of trying—maybe FOREVER."

Louisa Belinda had heard the rumors.
She considered for a moment.
She had lovely eyes; and how would she eat with a closed-up jaw?
But Joe's eyes did not bulge. His jaw had not closed up.
And she could balance the length of a fallen log,
just the same as he could.

Nervous, she said anyway,
"I was born to ride."

Joe was a good teacher—
patient, and clear in giving
instructions.

Even so,
Louisa Belinda fell.

And fell again.

And again.

And again.

And again.

Joe said, "Want to call it a day?"

Louisa Belinda hurt all over. She touched
her eyes, tested her jaw. "How's my face?"

"Same as ever," Joe said.
Louisa Belinda sighed, relieved.

A very large part of her wanted to give up,
to go inside for tea and cake and a hot bath.
But if she gave up now, would she ever try again?

So she said, "I will ride."

She hopped back on,

wobbled,

then, lo! She rode!

With some alarm, she felt her eyes bulge,
and her mouth widen—

into a **gigantic, joyous smile.**

Like a bird in flight,
she soared over the hill.

Like a fox on the prairie,
she skimmed the ground.

Like a bear, she roared,
"Hello, world! This is my bicycle face!"

"Those pants seem quite practical, Louisa Belinda," said Mother.

"They are!"

"Joe, dear," said Mother. "Is Father's bicycle in good riding condition?"

"Tip-top condition."

Louisa Belinda grinned.

"Mother," she said, "what will *your* bicycle face be, I wonder!"

About Bicycle Face

By the 1890s, people were wild for bicycles. Bicycle madness had taken over the country and even those who didn't ride were eager to talk about everything relating to the bicycle wheel.

Two topics in particular generated a lot of enthusiasm. Perhaps the most fervid conversations centered on women cyclists, known as *wheelwomen*, who rode in the face of convention. But another subject also drummed up intense debate. Was bicycling dangerous to one's health? Cyclists, especially wheelwomen, were cautioned to guard against afflictions such as *bicycle leg*, *bicycle hump*, and *bicycle face*.

Bicycle face, it was said, came from the strain of staying balanced and focused on the road. Supposedly, you could tell when people had bicycle face by the way their eyes bulged and how their jaws tightened. While anyone might acquire a bicycle affliction, bicycle face was disproportionately applied to women, and with particular meanness.

THE BICYCLE—THE GREAT DRESS REFORMER OF THE NINETEENTH CENTURY!

The bicycle—the great dress reformer of the nineteenth century!
(Illustration from *Puck*, 1895, artist: Ehrhart, S. D., Library of Congress.)

You see, not everyone approved of women riding bicycles. Women were expected to be pretty, demure, and domestic; but wheelwomen often contradicted these perceptions. Many people publicly (sometimes viciously) scolded women for bicycling—calling it improper, a direct challenge to the male sphere, and dangerous to women's health. Saying a woman had bicycle face was an attempt to intimidate and shame her, and, ultimately, keep her from the wheel.

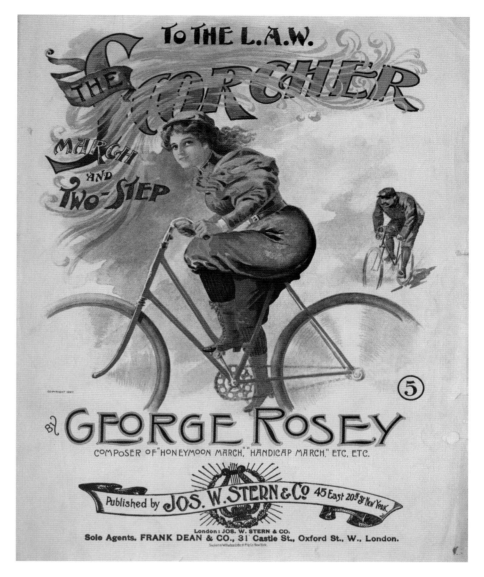

"The Scorcher." A "scorcher" was a bicyclist who leaned forward and rode hard and fast just for the thrill of it. (David M. Rubenstein Rare Book & Manuscript Library at Duke University.)

Fortunately, wheel-women ignored their critics. They formed clubs and opened cafés where they could meet in safety and peace. They established a magazine called *The Wheelwoman*. They taught one another how to fix their own bicycles. They competed in races and broke records. They adjusted their fashion so they could ride unrestricted, wearing shorter skirts and loose-fitting pants called bloomers, with functional pockets to hold a whistle, a handkerchief, and a few small tools.

Bicycling was a fun and speedy mode of transportation granting women greater freedom to exercise, socialize, travel, and work; and no threat of bicycle face could keep them from the wheel. Like Louisa Belinda, wheelwomen knew that a true bicycle face is one of joy.

From Bicycles to Votes

During the bicycle craze of the 1890s, bicycling was just one of many freedoms sought by women. Women also wanted access to education, sought personal and financial independence, were career-minded, had opinions and voiced them. And, women wanted to vote.

Messenger girl for the National Women's Party, 1922. (National Photo Company Collection, Library of Congress.)

Women had no representation and no voice in government—which was made up only of men who passed laws controlling and restricting women's rights and freedoms. The women's suffrage movement was a brave and necessary struggle against oppression. But it also spanned decades and was indefensibly segregated. Racially inclusive suffragist gatherings, like the one portrayed in Louisa Belinda's home, were rare. Powerful voices that influenced the slow-moving movement included those of Lucretia Mott, Sojourner Truth, Lucy Stone, Susan B. Anthony, Josephine St. Pierre Ruffin, and Ida B. Wells.

Despite setbacks and sometimes violent resistance, women organized and persisted, and won the right to vote in 1920 when the Nineteenth Amendment was ratified. However, state-sanctioned voter suppression tactics kept many women (and men) of color from the ballot box; and not until the Voting Rights Act of 1965 were all people of age guaranteed the right to vote without impediment. To this day, the right to vote in a free and fair election is one we fight to retain, not only for ourselves, but also for our neighbors.

Whether we're learning to ride a bike, facing insults for realizing our dreams, or championing our rights, there will always be times when we fall down and get hurt. When that happens, the thing that matters most is what we do next—can you guess what that should be? You got it—we get back up and try again. And maybe again. And probably again after that, until we truly learn to ride.

Bicycles afforded young people freedom to socialize without chaperones. (Charles S. Lillybridge, Ph.00259, Scan20000294, History Colorado.)